# *Noel's*
## Almost-Perfect
## Just-About-Wonderful
# Christmas

*for Janet Thoma*

Published in Nashville, Tennessee, by Thomas Nelson, Inc., Publishers, and distributed in Canada by Word Communications, Ltd., Richmond, British Columbia.

The Bible version used in this publication is THE NEW KING JAMES VER-SION. Copyright © 1979, 1980, 1982 Thomas Nelson, Inc., Publishers.

ISBN 0-7852-8194-0

Printed in the United States of America

2  3  4  5  6  –  99  98  97  96  95

# *Noel's* Almost-Perfect Just-About-Wonderful Christmas

**Mary Manz Simon**

*Illustrated by* **Toni Wall**

THOMAS NELSON PUBLISHERS
Nashville • Atlanta • London • Vancouver

4

This Christmas was going to be the best Christmas ever. Noel just knew it. She was going to be the talking angel in the Christmas Eve program.

All the angels would sing, "Gloria." All the angels would wear

white wings and gold waistbands. But Noel would be the only one with a golden halo. Noel would be the only one to tell the shepherds the good news of Jesus' birth.

And best of all Grandma was coming to see the Christmas play.

Noel didn't mind going to bed the week before Christmas. This was the time of the Christmas parade. Noel would pick out a song to sing before prayers. Then she would take an animal to the manger to give to the baby Jesus for His birthday.

   This night, Noel and her mom sang, "Hark! the Herald Angels Sing." Then she put her rabbit, the one with a floppy ear, in front of the manger. The first animal in the Christmas parade.

   "Only four more days until the perfect Christmas," Noel said before she went to bed.

The next day was the last practice for the play, and Noel wanted to learn her part perfectly. "For there is born to you this day in the city of David a Savior, who is Christ the Lord," Noel mumbled over and over again as she got dressed.

"For today there is . . . Mommy, I'm getting scared. I can't make a mistake."

"You'll do fine," her mother assured her.

9

Once they got to church Noel asked, "Where's my halo?"

"Right here in the bag," Mother said. "Now relax, and enjoy yourself."

And Noel did have good time. She loved being the talking angel; she spoke the words perfectly. "For there is born to you this day in the city of David a Savior, who is Christ the Lord. And this will be the sign to you. . . ."

12

That night Noel put an old gray donkey in front of the manger. The second animal in the Christmas parade.

"Only three more days until the perfect Christmas," Noel said before she went to bed.

The next morning Noel helped her mom put the lights on the Christmas tree. "For there is born to you . . . ," she repeated over and over again as she wrapped the lights around and around the Christmas tree.

That night Noel put her favorite white bear, the one with soft pink paws and fur inside the ears, in front of the manger. The third animal in the Christmas parade.

"Only two more days until the perfect Christmas," Noel said before she went to bed.

The next day Noel was so excited she couldn't stand still. "Tomorrow is Christmas Eve," she reminded her mother. "Tomorrow Grandma comes. Tomorrow I'm the talking angel. I can't wait for the perfect Christmas."

That day Noel helped wrap last-minute presents. That day she shook some packages labeled "Noel." That day she sampled cookie dough. That night Noel put her teeny-tiny teddy bear in front of the manger. The fourth animal in the Christmas parade. "Only one more day until the perfect Christmas," Noel said before she went to bed. Tomorrow Grandma would see her manger parade.

The next morning it was raining outside when Noel woke up. Usually she didn't like rain, but today was Christmas Eve. Any weather was fine today. Grandma would come today. And tonight Grandma would watch Noel be the talking angel.

Noel practiced her lines over and over again. "For there is born to you this day in the city of David a Savior, who is Christ the Lord. And this will be the sign to you: you will find a Babe wrapped in swaddling cloths. . ." She concentrated so hard, she didn't hear the phone ring.

"Yes, I understand," Noel's mom spoke into the phone. "You're sure she'll be alright?"

Noel came around the corner to listen. She noticed that Mom looked worried.

Mom hung up the phone. "Noel," she said. "I've got some bad news. That was Aunt Ruth. Grandma tripped and fell last night. She broke her hip and is in the hospital. She'll be alright, but—"

"You mean Grandma can't come?" Noel's voice got louder. "You mean Grandma can't come for Christmas! She can't see me be the talking angel?"

"No," her mother said. "Grandma will be in the hospital for at least a week."

"That's not fair!" Noel yelled. "This was supposed to be the perfect Christmas. I'm the talking angel."

Noel ran to her room and slammed the door. It banged so hard, some animals fell down in front of the manger.

In a few minutes Mom came in. She sat down on the bed and stroked Noel's hair.

"I hate Grandma," Noel said. "She ruined Christmas. She ruined my perfect Christmas."

Noel's mother spoke gently. "I know you're disappointed. But remember, Grandma didn't want to fall down. It was an accident."

"I don't want to go without Grandma. It won't be perfect," said Noel.

"Noel, you have an important job as the talking angel. You will tell others about Jesus. *You've got to go.*"

Noel thought about her not-so-perfect Christmas. The rain outside *tap-tap-tapped* on the window.

A half hour later Mother called from the doorway. "Time to eat, sweetheart. The talking angel can't be late."

Noel got up slowly. "It's not going to be a perfect Christmas," she said.

"That first Christmas probably didn't seem so perfect, either," Noel's mother reminded her. "Poor Mary and Joseph didn't even have a warm bed for their baby. Baby Jesus had to sleep with cows.

"But even though it was not-so-perfect, they went ahead. And you need to, too. You need to tell others about Jesus."

At church the air was filled with excitement. All of a sudden Noel got scared. She had been so upset, she had forgotten to review her part!

Now it was time for the talking angel to speak those familiar words. Mrs. Brown, the director, nudged her forward.

"For there is born to you this day in the city of David a Savior, who is Christ the Lord. And this will be the sign to you: you will find a Babe wrapped in swaddling cloths, lying in a manger." The talking angel spoke her lines perfectly.

After the program was over, Noel's mother gave her a warm hug. "Oh, darling, you were wonderful. I'm so proud of you."

"It's a happy Christmas and a not-so-happy Christmas," Noel said. "It's not a perfect Christmas, but that's okay."

Mother nodded. "We have the one thing we need for Christmas," she said. "All we need to know is that Jesus, our Savior, was born. You said that tonight and now everybody knows."

"Come on, honey," said Mother. "Let's go call Grandma at the hospital and tell her about tonight. You can be her very own talking angel."

Noel reached up to hug her mom. "I love you, Mommy," she said. "This is an almost-perfect, just-about wonderful Christmas."

# NOTE TO ADULT

Christmas is a time for traditions. People and places change through the years, but traditions span generations and miles.

With the approach of the holiday season, we once again have the opportunity to practice Christ-centered traditions. Your family, like ours, might gather together to sing carols and songs after supper each night during December. Or, like Noel in this story, your child might bring personal gifts of love to the Christ child during the days before Christmas.

In whatever ways you choose to celebrate, have a blessed celebration of Jesus' birth.